Hooray for Reading!

For my mom—who made reading an adventure
for hundreds of kids —P. H.

SIMON SPOTLIGHT
An imprint of Simon & Schuster Children's Publishing Division
1230 Avenue of the Americas
New York, New York 10020
This Simon Spotlight edition October 2015
For information about special discounts for bulk purchases, please contact Simon & Schuster Special Sales at
1-866-506-1949 or business@simonandschuster.com
Manufactured in the United States of America 0915 LAK
2 4 6 8 10 9 7 5 3 1
Library of Congress Cataloging-in-Publication Data
Hall, Patricia, 1948-
Hooray for reading! / by Patricia Hall ; illustrated by Kathryn Mitter.—1st ed.
p. cm. — (Classic Raggedy Ann & Andy) (Ready-to-read)
Summary: Marcella is learning how to read, and her dolls want to learn too.
[1. Reading—Fiction. 2. Dolls—Fiction.] I. Mitter, Kathy, ill. II. Title. III. Series.
IV. Series: Ready-to-read
PZ7.H147515 Ho 2002
[E]—dc21
2002000942
ISBN 978-1-4814-5080-5 (hc)
ISBN 978-1-4814-5079-9 (pbk)
ISBN 978-1-4814-5081-2 (eBook)
RaggedyAnnBooks.com

RAGGEDY ANN & ANDY
Hooray for Reading!

by Patricia Hall
illustrated by Kathryn Mitter

Ready-to-Read

Simon Spotlight
New York   London   Toronto   Sydney   New Delhi

Marcella came home
from her first day
of school.
She was excited.

"I am learning to read!"
she told Raggedy Ann
and Raggedy Andy.

"Let me show you
how I can read,"
Marcella said.

She sat her dolls in rows.
Then she held up cards.

"Apple," said Marcella,
"and Ant.

These words begin with A."

Marcella held up
two more cards.

"Baby and Ball," she said.
"These are B words."

Marcella held up more cards.
She read more words.

"Isn't learning to read fun?"
asked Marcella.
Then she went outside to play.

"Did you hear?"
asked Cleety the Clown.
"She knew all the words!"
said Frederika.

"Marcella is very smart!"
said the Camel
with the Wrinkled Knees.

"Reading is an adventure,"
said Raggedy Ann,
"I love to read."
"I love adventures!"
said Raggedy Andy.

"Can you help us
learn to read, Raggedy Ann?"
the dolls asked.

Raggedy Ann found a crayon.
She drew on some cards.

"Take your seats,"
she said.
"School is starting!"

Raggedy Ann held two cards.
"Here are two A words,"
she said.

"Here are words
that start with B.
Bunny and Brown Bear!"
said Eddie Elephant.

"Look what begins with C!"
said Raggedy Ann.
"Camel!" giggled Uncle Clem.
"Clem!" laughed
the Camel with the Wrinkled Knees.

"How about some D words?"
asked Raggedy Ann.
"Doll, Duck, and Danny
Daddles!" said Frederika.

"Here come some E words!"
sang Raggedy Ann.
"Eddie and Elephant!"
said Raggedy Andy.

"What begins with F?"
asked Raggedy Ann.
"Fido!"
laughed Raggedy Andy.
"And Frederika, too!"

"Hooray for reading!"
But then—
Blump! Clump! Blump!

The dolls fell off the bed
and the cards flew
everywhere!

"Oh, my," sighed Uncle Clem.
"Learning to read
is an adventure!"
"And a mess,"
said Raggedy Andy.

"Don't worry,"
said Raggedy Ann.
"We know our alphabet now.
We can stack the cards
by their letters."

Soon the playroom
was neat again.
Then in came Marcella.

"Today we read
a real book at school!"
she said.
"It was an adventure story!"

"You cannot really read,"
said Marcella.
"But maybe someday—
you can have
a reading adventure too!"